THE ELECTROMAGNETIC SPECTRUM

UNDERSTANDING AND USING VISIBLE LIGHT

ELIZABETH RUBIO

Enslow PUBLISHING

Published in 2022 by Enslow Publishing, LLC.
101 W. 23rd Street, Suite 240, New York, NY 10011

Library of Congress Cataloging-in-Publication Data

Names: Rubio, Elizabeth, author.
Title: Understanding and using visible light / Elizabeth Rubio.
Description: New York, NY : Enslow Publishing, LLC., 2022 | Series: The electromagnetic spectrum | Includes bibliographical references and index. | Audience: 7–12.
Identifiers: LCCN 2019008950| ISBN 9781978514980 (library bound) | ISBN 9781978514973 (pbk.) |
Subjects: LCSH: Light—Juvenile literature.
Classification: LCC QC360 .R83 2022 | DDC 535—dc23
LC record available at https://lccn.loc.gov/2019008950

Printed in the United States of America

To Our Readers: We have done our best to make sure all websites in this book were active and appropriate when we went to press. However, the author and the publisher have no control over and assume no liability for the material available on those websites or on any websites they may link to. Any comments or suggestions can be sent by email to customerservice@enslow.com.

Photos Credits: Cover kmis/Shutterstock.com; p. 5 © iStockphoto.com/kasezo; p. 8, 9 VectorMine/Shutterstock.com; p. 12 NASA/Hulton Archive/Getty Images; p. 15 Corbis Historical/Getty Images; p. 19 udaix/Shutterstock.com; p. 21 Dorling Kindersley/Getty Images; pp. 25, 33 Peter Hermes Furian/Shutterstock.com; pp. 26, 29 Fouad A. Saad/Shutterstock.com; p. 32 solar22/Shutterstock.com; p. 35 eveleen/Shutterstock.com; p. 37 AboutLife/Shutterstock.com; p. 40 Romolo Tavani/Shutterstock.com; p. 43 Paulo Oliveira/Alamy Stock Photo; p. 44 world-classphoto/Shutterstock.com; p. 47 Wayhome studio/Shutterstock.com (all); p. 48 Heritage Images/Hulton Fine Art Collection/Getty Images; p. 50 Elena Voynova/Shutterstock.com; p. 51 Andrey Korshenkov/Shutterstock.com; p. 54 Macrovector/Shutterstock.com; cover background, interior pages (faceted color pattern) s_maria/Shutterstock.com; interior pages (wave graphic) MagicMary/Shutterstock.com

CONTENTS

INTRODUCTION

Every day people use visible light to navigate the world. Sight, one of the senses upon which humans rely, depends on visible light. When a person checks their clothes in a mirror, reads a book, watches a movie, or hits a baseball, they are using visible light.

The story of visible light is an old one. Long before humans existed, animals relied on visible light in much the same ways people do today. Even plants have light receptors that help them sense daylight and distinguish it from night.

But today's understanding of light was not easy to come by. For thousands of years, many great thinkers, including Plato, Newton, and Einstein, have wondered just how light works and have performed experiments to find out. Thanks to their contributions, along with those of others, we now understand what light is, how it works, and what it can do.

Light is remarkable because, unlike matter made of particles or sound made of waves, light has properties of both particles *and* waves. This means that it can interact with objects in very much the same way matter can—light can change the properties of matter and even be pulled by gravity. It can also get around objects the way waves can—light can flow over an object like a ripple in a pond flows over a stone.

Light, as most people know, reflects, or bounces off objects. But it can also be absorbed, or drawn into objects. It transmits, or goes through objects. It refracts, or bends. A special way that

A prism is a material that can split white light into all the colors contained in that light. Each color is a different wavelength.

light refracts is through a prism. A prism can refract each color of white light separately, splitting white light into all the colors of the rainbow. Rainbows themselves are the result of small drops of water in the atmosphere acting as prisms. Together, they create rainbows many miles across.

Visible light is just one type of light, but people rely on it in many ways. They use it to look at objects. Plants use visible light as energy to grow. Light is used for art, communication, and science. Light allows people to push the boundaries of what is possible, rendering 3D videos and interactive games. This can only be done because of our understanding of visible light and the way humans perceive it.

Some people have difficulty seeing light properly. Some people are nearsighted and cannot see distant objects clearly, while others are farsighted and cannot see close objects clearly. Luckily, these conditions are easily corrected with lenses, such as glasses or contact lenses. A smaller number of people cannot see colors correctly—for example, people with a certain type of color blindness cannot distinguish between red and green. Even color blindness can now be corrected with special lenses that alter the way light enters the eye. The more that is known about difficulties people have perceiving light, the more it is possible to help people overcome those difficulties.

CHAPTER ONE

THE ELECTROMAGNETIC SPECTRUM

The word "radiation" sounds scary. When people hear it, they may think of atom bombs and the enormous devastation they cause. But in truth, all light is a form of radiation. Visible light is just part of the spectrum of electromagnetic radiation. Not all radiation is harmful, and much of it is very useful, both to humans and to many other kinds of organisms as well.

What Is the Electromagnetic Spectrum?

The electromagnetic spectrum encompasses the entire range of electromagnetic radiation. This radiation includes all forms of light—not only visible light, but also radio waves, microwaves, X-rays, and gamma rays. Light is also called electromagnetic radiation because it is a wave of alternating electric and magnetic fields. Just like waves in the ocean, light travels in waves, spreading out in all directions from its source.

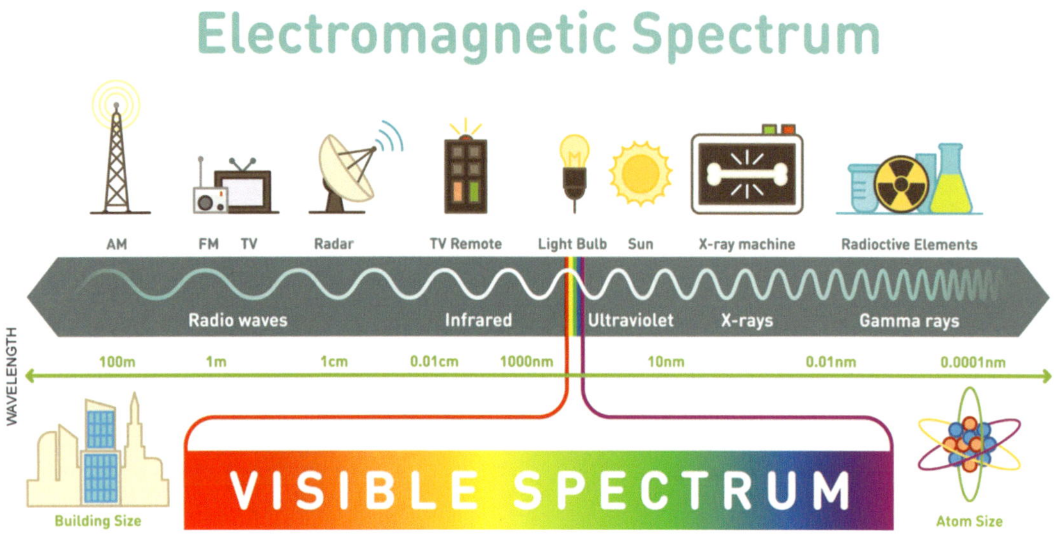

The electromagnetic spectrum encompasses all kinds of light. Visible light is only a tiny portion of this spectrum, and it lies between infrared and ultraviolet radiation.

Because light is made of waves, each type of light has a specific wavelength. A wavelength is the distance between two crests of a wave. Light with shorter wavelengths has more energy than light with longer wavelengths. Put another way, light with shorter wavelengths is more powerful and can penetrate more objects than light with longer wavelengths.

Wavelengths in the electromagnetic spectrum range from several kilometers (miles) on the low-energy end of the spectrum to 1×10^{-13} meters on the high-energy end. Put another way, the lowest energy light has a wavelength longer than a city block, and the highest energy light has a wavelength smaller than the diameter of an atom.

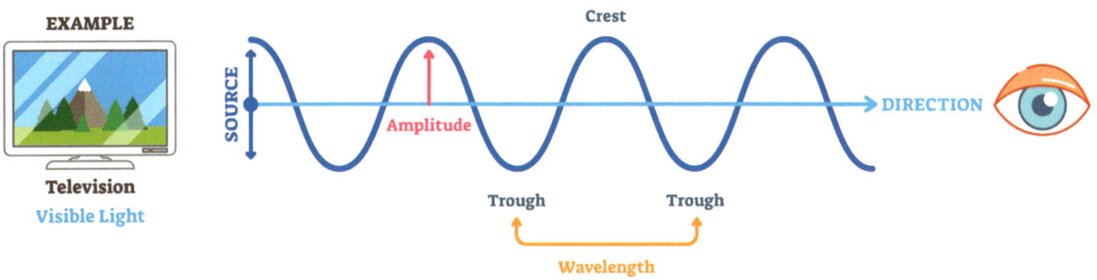

Amplitude is the height of the wave, measured as half the distance from the trough to the crest. Wavelength is the distance between crests or troughs.

How Does Visible Light Compare to Other Kinds of Light?

Visible light comprises the wavelengths from about 380 nanometers (nm) to about 700 nm.[1] Humans perceive each range of wavelengths as color: red, orange, yellow, green, blue, indigo, and violet. A common acronym used to remember the colors of light is ROY G BIV.

Just beyond the red wavelength is infrared, the wavelength used in heat-detecting cameras. Just beyond the violet wavelength is ultraviolet, the light from the sun that causes sunburns.

Visible light is non-ionizing radiation, meaning it cannot eject an electron from an atom. This makes it harmless. Ionizing radiation, which includes electromagnetic radiation of wavelengths shorter than those in the visible spectrum, can eject electrons from atoms and can therefore be harmful.

Emission of Light

People see the things around them because of visible light. But most objects do not emit visible light. Only things that look bright, such as light bulbs, flames, or the sun, emit light. Light is emitted after electrons in an atom become excited. When these electrons return to their normal, unexcited state, light is given off. Additionally, heat is given off, which is why all objects that emit light also emit heat. The amount of heat given off varies. For example, light-emitting diodes (LEDs) give off very little heat, while a burning log gives off a lot of heat.

The amount of light emitted by an object can be measured. This is called brightness or luminosity. Often, it is important to know the luminosity of a light when used for a specific purpose. For example, there are legal limits on the luminosity of headlights on vehicles. These limits exist so that a vehicle's headlights do not shine so brightly that they temporarily blind drivers in oncoming traffic. Other times, people simply want to control the brightness of lighting. People may prefer brighter lights in rooms where they do activities such as reading or making art. Conversely, they may prefer dimmer lights in rooms where they do activities such as watching television or sleeping.

A major source of light for Earth is the sun. The sun emits a great deal of light and heat. Some people refer to the sun as a ball of burning gas, but this is not correct. In fact, the sun is made of plasma, a very dense form of matter. Although plasma is rarely found on Earth, it is very common in the universe because all stars are made of plasma. Plasma has a

EMISSION AND REFLECTION

Emission and reflection of light are two of the important phenomena that allow us to see the world. Would you like to try some experiments with emission and reflection of light?

Choose a room with a mirror that can be made completely or mostly dark, such as a bathroom. Turn off the lights and turn on a flashlight. Shine the light toward the mirror. What happens? How does the flashlight beam change if you change the angle of the flashlight compared to the mirror?

Challenge: See if you can shine the flashlight beam on a particular object by reflecting it off the mirror. Try for an object above yourself, to the right of yourself, and to the left of yourself.

great deal of energy, which is why the sun gives off so much light and heat. In fact, the sun is more like a giant nuclear reactor than a ball of burning gas!

At night, when the sun is on the other side of Earth, things are much darker. This is because Earth itself blocks most of the light from the sun. The stars are visible at night because the sun's rays do not interfere with our ability to see them. Distant stars emit light constantly, but during the day we cannot see them because the sun's light is so bright it makes it hard to see anything else.

The moon is visible both at night and during the day. The term "moonlight" might be familiar, but in fact, the moon does not emit light at all. The moon appears bright because it reflects

"Moonlight" is just the sun's light reflected off the surface of the moon. On the moon, Earth appears bright and colorful because it also reflects the sun's light.

light emitted by the sun. From the surface of the moon, Earth appears very bright for the exact same reason.

Reflection makes many people think of mirrors, but in fact, all visible objects reflect some light. When light strikes an object, some or all of it bounces off the object's surface. This is reflection. The amount of light that bounces off the surface depends on how reflective the surface is. Mirrors are highly reflective, so almost all light that strikes them bounces back off.

CHAPTER TWO

THE HISTORY OF LIGHT

What is light? The answer seems both obvious and mysterious. Light is what allows us to see. But is it an object? A form of energy? A wave?

People have been wondering about light for thousands of years. As far back as ancient Greece, Plato worked to develop a theory of light and vision. His idea, that the eyes emitted "vision beams," seems laughable now, but the tools he had to study light were less advanced than those we have today. As technology progressed, so too did our collective understanding of light.

Early Discoveries and Ideas

In ancient Greece, philosopher-scientists thought a great deal about light. They were largely concerned with vision and the way the eye perceives light. There were several competing ideas about the phenomenon of vision. Democritus, who lived from 460 to 370 BCE, believed that the image of an object arose from the air between the object and the eye being compressed and "stamped" with the object's image. Epicurus, who lived from 341 to 270 BCE, proposed that particles flowed continuously from objects into the eye.

Plato, who lived from 428 to 348 BCE, developed what became known as the essence of extramission theory of light. This theory stated that the eyes emitted rays in the direction of sight. The rays struck objects and allowed them to be seen. Vision was limited by the distance these rays could reach. Plato's theory proved extremely popular and persisted for the next 1,000 years.

While these thinkers were developing ideas about vision, mathematician-scientists were developing mathematical principles to describe light. Euclid, who lived from about 370 to about 250 BCE and was known as the father of geometry, developed sets of mathematical formulae to describe the angles of reflection involved in vision. Claudius Ptolemy, who lived from 90 to 168 CE, wrote a book called *Optics* that laid out a mathematical theory of vision, reflection, refraction, and optical illusion. Perhaps surprisingly, both Euclid and Ptolemy were adherents of Plato's extramission theory.

For about a thousand years after these ideas were put forward, little progress was made in humanity's understanding of light. The Islamic Golden Age, which began in the eighth century CE, saw the first challenges to Plato's extramission theory. A number of scholars, including Muhammad ibn Zakariya al-Razi, Abu Nasr Muhammad al-Farabi, and Abu 'Ali al-Husayn ibn Sina, objected to the theory, citing experimental and mathematical evidence that did not support it.

Abu Sad Al Alla Ibn Sahl, who lived from 940 to 1000 CE, developed a law of refraction by analyzing the way light bent

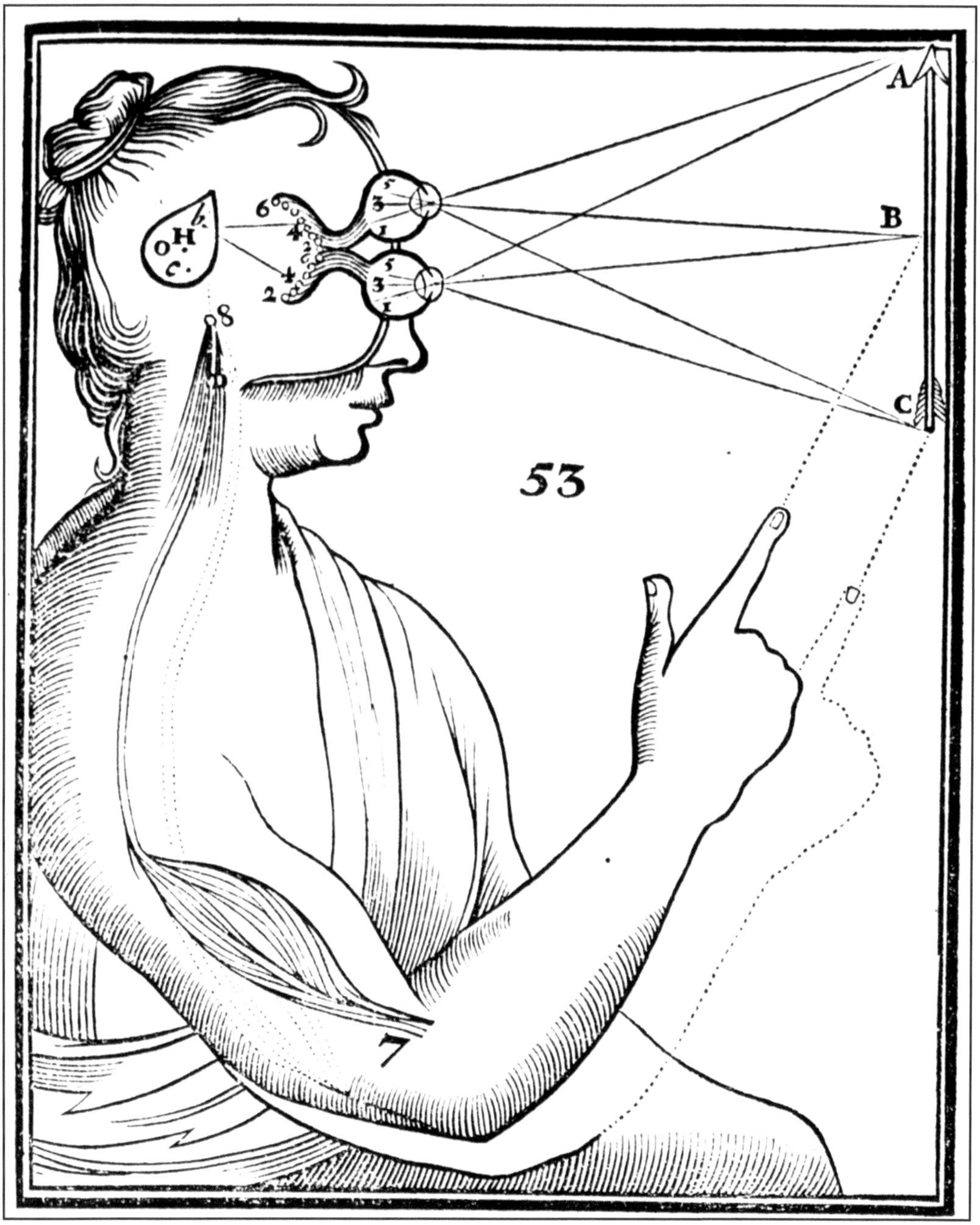

René Descartes, a French mathematician, and scientist, drew this diagram of Plato's extramission theory of light, which suggested that the eyes emitted beams that allowed them to see.

through lenses and when reflected by mirrors. Six hundred years later, Dutch scientist Willebrord Snellius developed these same laws, which the Western world then recognized. Only recently has Ibn Sahl received proper credit for the discovery.

Abu Ali al-Hasan ibn al-Hasan ibn al-Haytham, who lived from 965 to 1040 and was known in the West as Alhazen, made what was probably the last of the great advances in the early science of light. His book *Kitab al-Manzir* (Book of Optics) was the definitive authority on optics until Isaac Newton published his own work in 1704. Alhazen showed with experimental evidence that the concepts and equations put forth by Euclid and Ptolemy held true. He invented the first pinhole camera and explained why the image generated by

PINHOLE CAMERA

A pinhole camera is just what it sounds like—a box that uses a pinhole to make an image. The first pinhole cameras did not capture photos because photo paper had not yet been invented. Instead, people simply put their heads into the camera and looked at the image inside it.

Today, anyone can make a simple pinhole camera with a few common objects. A dark box with a hole, a thin sheet of metal with a tiny hole made by a pin, and a piece of photo paper are all that is required. However, the photo paper must be developed in harsh chemicals, so most people use digital cameras instead.

the camera was upside down. Alhazen additionally generated a mathematical problem involving the angles of reflection and refraction on the surface of a curved mirror that was not solved until 1997.

Modern Discoveries in Light

For centuries after Alhazen published *Kitab al-Manzir*, little progress was made. In 1615, Willebrord Snellius published the laws of refraction previously determined by Ibn Sahl, which are now known as Snell's law.

The first major new ideas were conceived by Isaac Newton in the late seventeenth century. Newton made many contributions to the field of optics, including discoveries about color being a property of light rather than the medium through which light passes. Newton also designed a reflecting telescope that eliminated many of the distortions common to previous refracting telescopes.

Newton also supported the corpuscular theory of light, first put forth by philosopher René Descartes. He believed that light was composed of tiny particles he called "corpuscles." He reasoned that waves could not travel in straight lines, as light clearly did, and therefore light must be made up of small particles.[1]

Around the same time, Christiaan Huygens set out to show that light was made of waves. Critics had pointed out a major flaw in Newton's corpuscular theory: if light were made of particles, diffraction, such as the blurry edges of shadows, would not occur. Huygens suggested that light was made of longitudinal waves (the same type as sound waves), which propagated through an "ether" in the air. At the time, Newton's theory received more support than Huygens's.

Thomas Young, who was born a century after Huygens published his wave theory of light, set out to show that wave theory was correct.[2] He first demonstrated wave interference using a tank full of water and then showed that light waves demonstrate interference with the famous double-slit experiment. He went on to show that light behaves as a wave with many other experiments in diffraction and reflection.

A major breakthrough came in the late nineteenth century when James Clerk Maxwell showed that light, magnetism, and electricity are all aspects of the same phenomenon, which he dubbed electromagnetism. He set out a series of equations that could be used to predict the movement of waves of an electrical field and declared that they applied to light as well.

The debate became further muddled when Max Planck determined that light could be emitted only in discrete amounts of energy. This unusual idea became the basis for quantum physics, a new field that would emerge.

In the early twentieth century, Albert Einstein expanded on Planck's theory by demonstrating the photoelectric effect, the phenomenon by which light can cause electrons to be emitted from a material. If Planck had been incorrect, dim lighting would show a slowed photoelectric effect compared to bright lighting, because the energy required to release an electron would have to build over time. This was not the case—electrons are released only when the energy threshold is reached, and no amount of continuous light below this threshold will result in the effect. This cemented the knowledge that light consists of discrete packets.

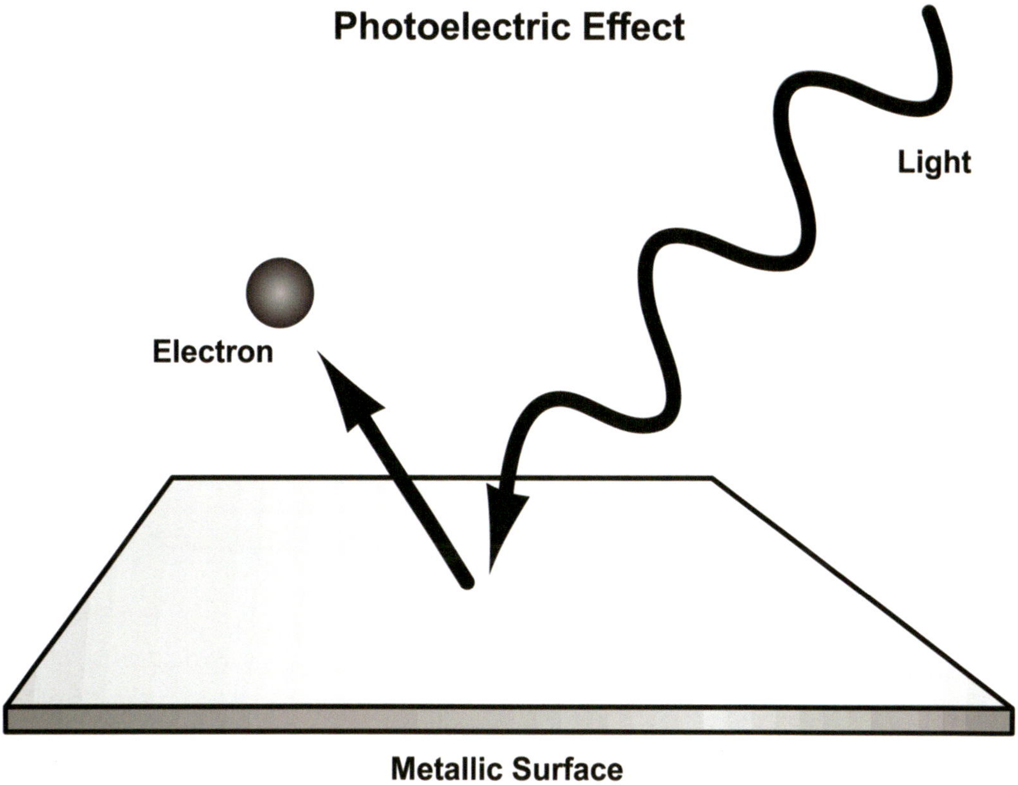

The photoelectric effect describes the emission of an electron from a material when light strikes it. Its discovery led to an understanding of quantum physics.

Wave-Particle Duality of Light

For decades, debate raged among scientists about whether light was a wave or a particle. Some, such as Huygens and Young, declared that light was a wave and showed experimental data supporting their claims. Others, such as Newton and Planck, declared that light was a discrete particle and showed experimental data supporting their claims. How could the data support these competing claims?

The undeniable evidence for light behaving as both a wave and a particle led, in the twentieth century, to the acceptance of the wave-particle duality of light. Light behaves as *both* a wave and a particle. This is known as the wave-particle duality of light. To be clear, light does not sometimes behave like a wave and other times like a particle. Light always behaves as both a wave and a particle.

The Double-Slit Experiment

Thomas Young was one of the leading researchers who set out to show that light is a wave. His most famous experiment is the double-slit experiment. In this experiment, Young positioned a light source in front of a screen containing two slits. Behind the screen was a second screen with no slits or holes. When light was emitted from the light source, it passed through the two slits and made a distinct pattern on the second screen. This pattern showed bands of light and shadow, with the brightest bands in the middle, dimming as they spread out from the center.[3]

The behavior of light as a wave explains these bands. Where the waves overlap, they cause brighter bands to appear on the second screen. This is similar to the way waves ripple out from pebbles dropped into a pool. Each pebble generates waves. Where the waves generated by the pebbles meet, they combine to form higher waves than either one individually.

In the years since Young published his experiment, it has been repeated time and time again, using not just light but

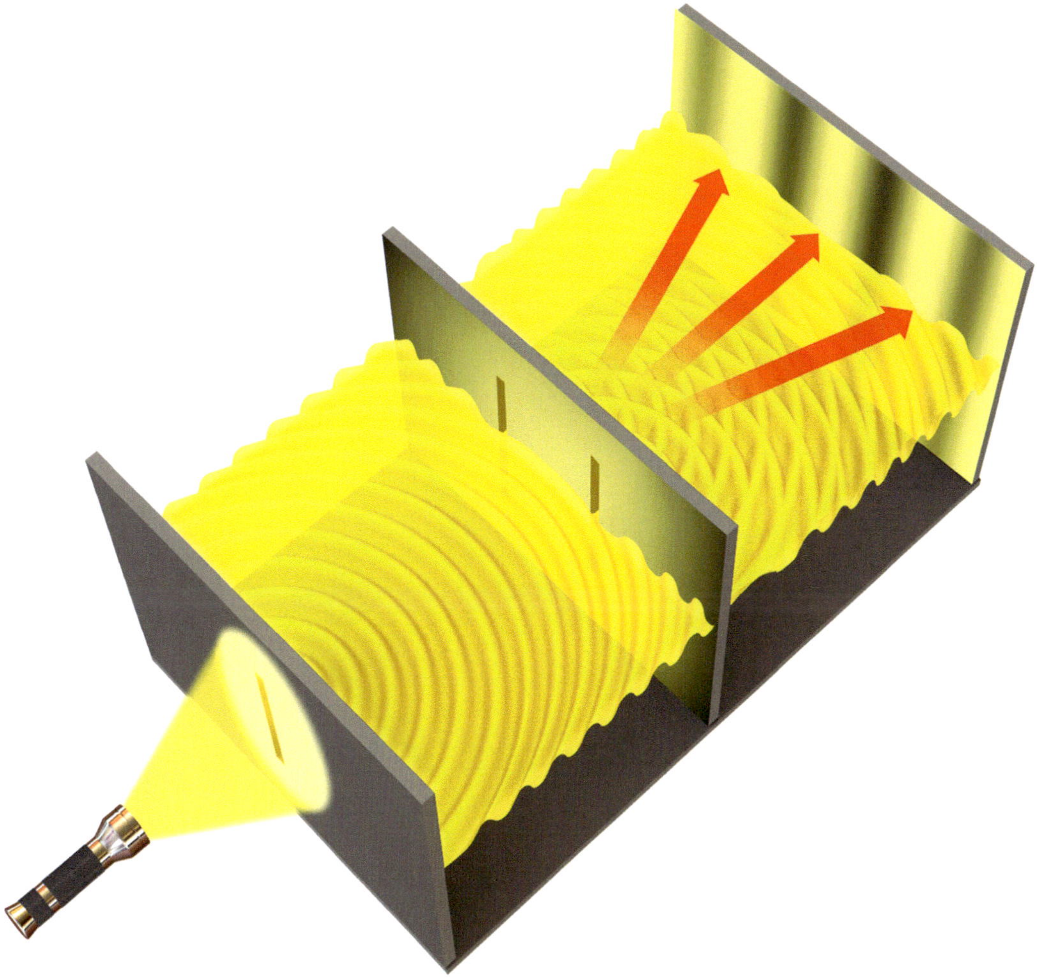

In the double-slit experiment, a beam of light passes through two small slits. The waves that exit these slits create a pattern of interference, captured on film as bright and dark bands.

also beams of electrons. The results continue to support his hypothesis—light behaves as a wave.

These observations, among others, showed that light has properties of both waves and particles. Light is not made of

THE DARKEST MATERIAL IN THE WORLD

When people think of a black object, they may think of a dark object such as a black ball. Yet most black objects still reflect a great deal of light—that's how we see them.

However, a company in the United Kingdom has invented the darkest material in the world, called Vantablack. Vantablack is made of carbon nanotubes. The material absorbs nearly all light—99.96 percent, to be exact.

People are still finding uses for Vantablack, but among the possibilities are thermal camouflage, or hiding from heat cameras, boosting thermal energy systems, and increasing telescope power.

atoms, as matter is, but its energy is not distributed across entire waveforms, like sound. Instead, light is unique, both a wave and a particle at all times. Whether light behaves as a wave or a particle depends entirely on the way it is measured. It propagates like a wave, spreading out in ripples from its source, just like sound. But its energy is contained in discrete units and cannot exist outside of these units, just like atoms.

THE VISIBLE SPECTRUM

CHAPTER THREE

The visible spectrum encompasses all the light humans can see. But just what exactly is the visible spectrum?

The visible spectrum occupies a very small portion of the entire electromagnetic spectrum. Its rays are not damaging because they have relatively long wavelengths, which means they have relatively low energy (as compared to, for example, X-rays, which can damage genetic material in cells).

Wavelengths and Color

The visible spectrum consists of light between roughly 380 nm to 700 nm. The shortest wavelengths are violet and the longest are red. This is why light with wavelengths just shorter than those in the visible spectrum is called ultraviolet, while light with wavelengths just longer than those in the visible spectrum is called infrared.

Violet light ranges between 380 and 425 nm. Indigo light ranges between 425 and 450 nm. Blue light ranges between 450 and 495 nm. Green light ranges between 495 and 570 nm. Yellow light ranges between 570 and 590 nm. Orange light ranges between 590 and 620 nm. Red light ranges between 620 and 700 nm.

Color	Wavelength
Violet	380–425 nm
Indigo	425–450 nm
Blue	450–495 nm
Green	495–570 nm
Yellow	570–590 nm
Orange	590–620 nm
Red	620–700 nm

Of course, many colors exist besides the seven described in the spectrum. The other colors are formed by two or more of the colors of the spectrum interacting. For example, the color magenta, a common color used in computer displays, results from adding blue and red light. Cyan, another color used in computer displays, similarly results from adding blue and green light.

WAVELENGTHS AND COLOR

Anyone can perform a simple experiment to see how light of different colors can combine to make new colors. You can even do it yourself!

Use two or three flashlights with green, red, and blue filters. If you cannot obtain filters, substitute colored cling wrap. Alternatively, use red, green, and blue LEDs.

Place one filter over each flashlight, each a different color. If you are using cling wrap, you may need two or three layers. In a dark room, shine the flashlights at the same spot. What colors do you observe? How do the colors change where they overlap?

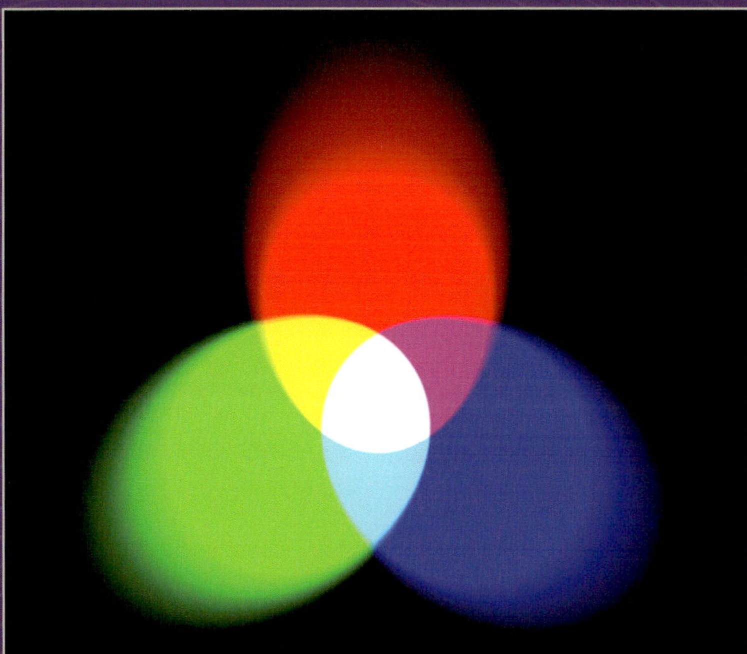

Light wave interference causes light of different colors to make a new color when shined at the same spot. Look closely at the places where the light beams overlap to find the different colors.

Absorption, Reflection, Transmission, and Refraction

Can you think of an object that reflects light? You're probably thinking of a mirror. However, almost all objects people can see reflect light. Mirrors are special in that they reflect *all* light.

Absorption occurs when light is absorbed by an object. In the case of light, this means the electrons of the object vibrate at exactly the same frequency as the light. When light strikes those electrons, they take in the energy of the light and transform it into thermal energy, also called heat. Importantly, this heat may not be so great that it can be felt with the fingers.

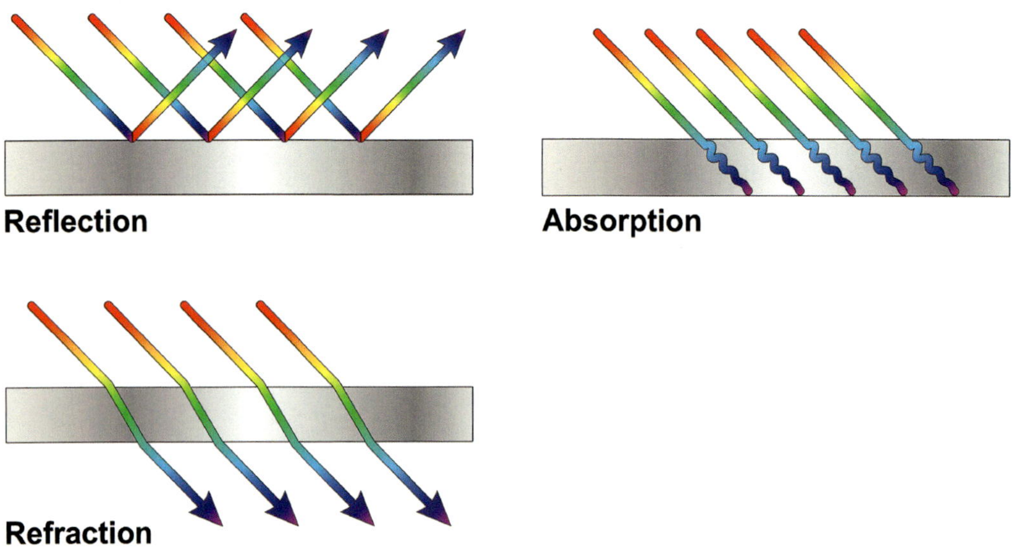

Reflection occurs when light bounces off a material. Absorption occurs when light is absorbed by the atoms of a material. Refraction occurs when light is bent as it passes through a material.

Reflection occurs when light bounces off an object. It is the opposite of absorption. Reflection and absorption together result in humans perceiving the color of objects.

For example, suppose you are looking at an orange. The fruit appears orange. This is because it reflects orange light, while absorbing all other colors. Similarly, a banana appears yellow because it reflects yellow light while absorbing all other colors.[2]

Transmission occurs when light passes through an object. For example, windows transmit nearly all light. Some materials transmit only some light, making them appear tinted or frosted. The degree to which a material allows light to pass through it is known as transmittance. Materials with high transmittance are transparent, while those with low transmittance are opaque.[3]

REFRACTION OF LIGHT

Refraction is easily noticed with media that have high transmittance, which means they are clear. For example, consider a straw in a clear glass of water. The straw seems to bend where it enters the water. This can be seen from above or from the side.

If the glass is thicker at the bottom, as many glasses are, the straw will appear thicker there too. The straw isn't changing where it enters the water or rests on the bottom of the glass. Refraction just makes it look that way.

Refraction occurs when light bends as it passes through a medium. A medium is any material that transmits light. This commonly happens with materials with high transmittance, such as water and glass. Refraction can redirect and even focus light waves. For example, the refraction that occurs in a microscope allows the user to focus the light so that the objects being viewed are distinct.[4]

Interference and Its Effects

Interference describes the phenomenon in which waves add together to change the total amplitude of the combined wave. Constructive interference occurs when the waves are in phase—that is, when the wave peaks are aligned exactly over each other. Constructive interference results in a wave with a larger amplitude than either individual wave. Destructive interference occurs when the waves are out of phase—that is, when the peak of one wave is aligned with the trough of the other. Destructive interference results in a wave with smaller amplitude than either individual wave, including, potentially, no amplitude at all.

For light waves, interference can change the color of the light. For example, green light (wavelengths from 495 to 570 nm) interferes with red light (wavelengths from 620 to 700 nm) to make yellow light (wavelengths from 570 to 590 nm).

Furthermore, interference causes patterns to appear when light of similar wavelengths passes through small openings or around objects. This formed the basis of Young's double-slit experiment. Additionally, following Young's experiment, other

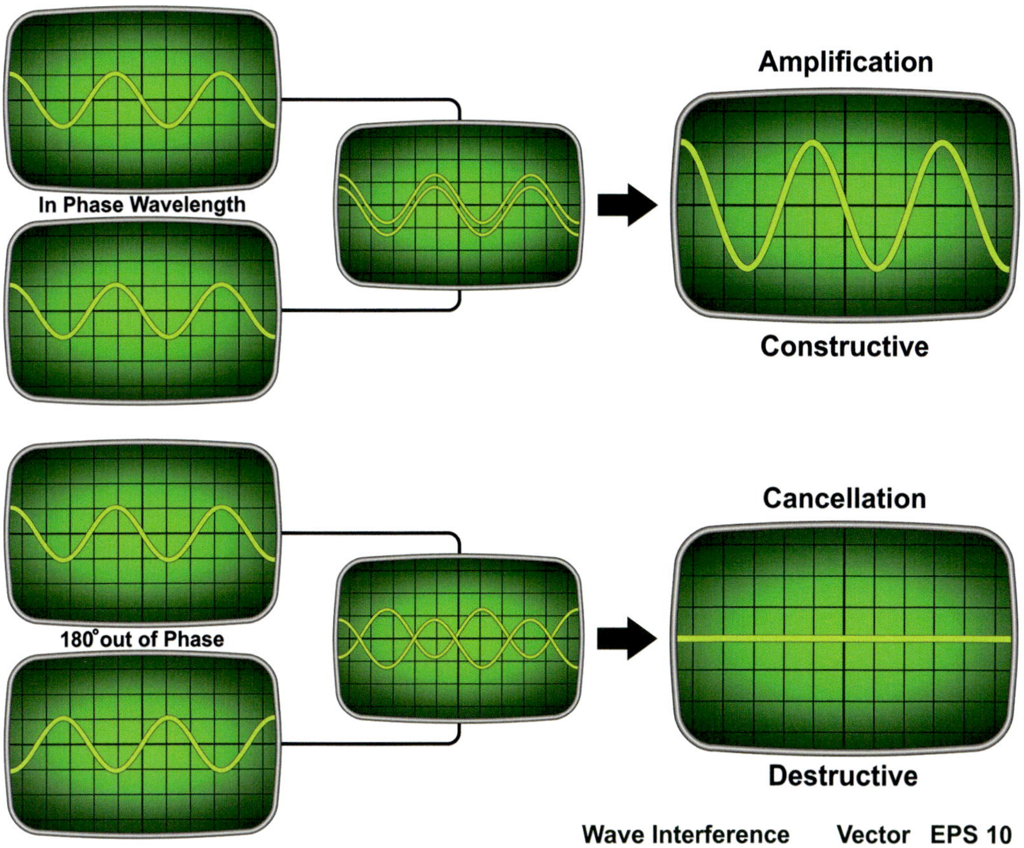

Wave Interference Vector EPS 10

Interference can be constructive or destructive. Constructive interference increases the amplitude of interfering waves, while destructive interference decreases their amplitude.

scientists began noticing interesting effects when light interacted with perfectly round objects. A bright spot, called an Arago spot, Poisson spot, or Fresnel bright spot, appears in the center of the shadow cast by a perfectly round object. This bright spot is the result of constructive interference of the light waves that propagate around the sphere. Similarly, alternating bright and dark rings appear around the edges of the shadow, much like the bands that appear in the double-slit experiment.

HUMAN PERCEPTION OF VISIBLE LIGHT

Visible light is so called because it is the light we humans can see. Just how do we see light? And what happens when things go wrong?

Light, the Eye, and the Brain

Human vision depends on both the eyes and the nervous system. The eye is a roughly spherical organ filled with a clear fluid called the vitreous humor. The front of the eye is the cornea, a clear window. Behind the cornea is the iris, the colored structure that expands and contracts to change the size of the pupil, which is the space through which light passes. Just behind the iris is the lens, which focuses light and can change shape to focus on near or far objects. The back of the eye is the retina. The retina contains photoreceptors, or light receptors, called rods and cones. The optic nerve extends from the back of the eye to the brain.

Human Eye Anatomy

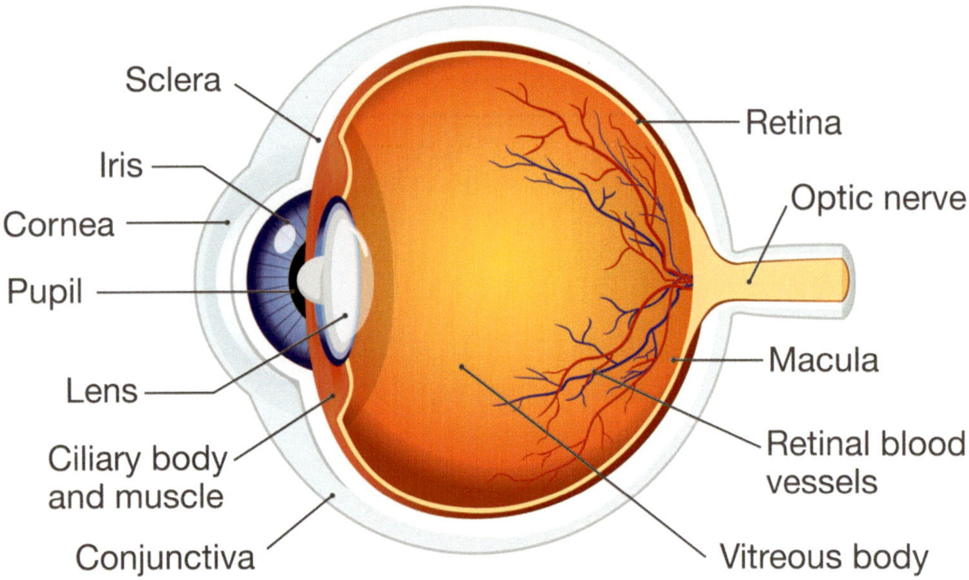

The human eye is highly specialized for vision. The parts of the eye must all work together to absorb light and transmit a signal to the brain, which interprets the signal as an image.

Vision relies on the interaction of light, the eye, and the brain. Light passes through the cornea to the lens. The iris expands or contracts to let more or less light in through the pupil, respectively, so that dim or bright scenes can be properly viewed. The lens focuses the light by expanding or contracting, to bring distant or close objects into focus. The focused light passes through the vitreous humor and strikes the retina, where it is absorbed by rods (which detect low light levels) and cones (which detect color).

There are three types of cones: short-wavelength cones (S), middle-wavelength cones (M), and long-wavelength cones (L). These cones absorb light in the short-, middle-, and long-wavelength ranges of the visible spectrum, respectively.

Once the photoreceptors have absorbed light, they transform the information into an electric impulse. This impulse travels along the optic nerve to the brain, where it is interpreted as an image. All of this takes the tiniest fraction of a second—0.15 second, in fact.[1]

Remarkably, the image the eye perceives is turned upside down within the vitreous humor due to the focusing effect of the lens. This upside-down image reaches the brain, which then interprets the image as rightside-up.

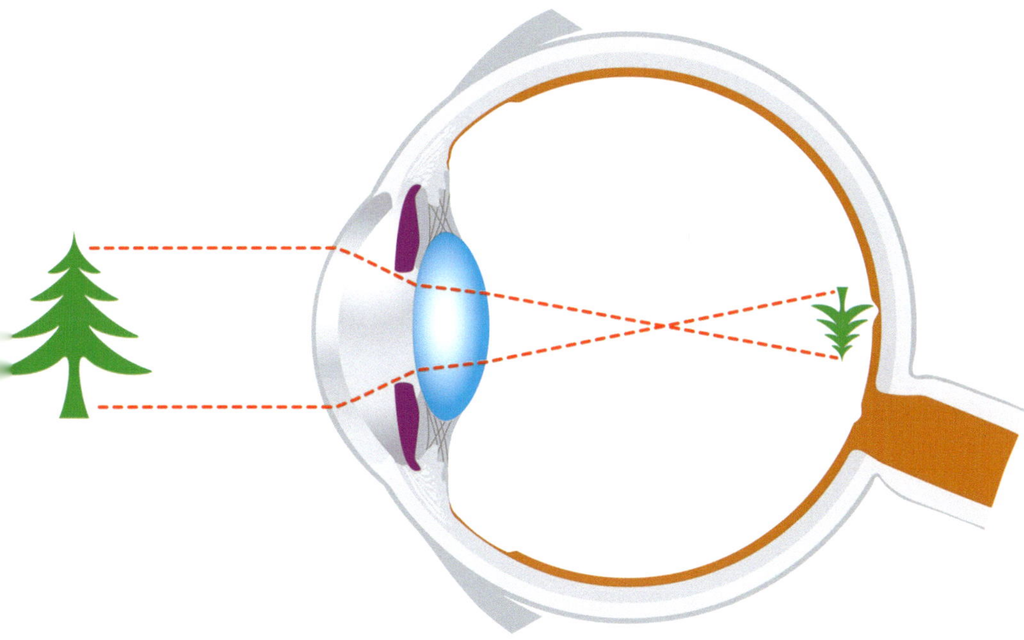

Light entering the eye is inverted, or turned upside down, when it passes through the vitreous humor. The brain interprets the upside-down image correctly.

Conditions Affecting Eyesight

When all works well, light enters the eye, is focused on the retina, and is transformed into signals interpreted by the brain. But sometimes, one or more parts of this pathway work improperly or do not work at all. The result is a visual deficiency.

The most common condition affecting eyesight is nearsightedness, or myopia. Myopia affects about 42 percent of Americans between ages 15 and 24.[2] Myopia is the result of elongation of the eye—the retina is too far away from the lens. Less commonly, a deformity of the cornea or lens can cause myopia. Myopia causes distant objects to appear blurry but has little effect on objects close to the eye. It can be corrected with concave lenses (either glasses or contact lenses).

Less common is farsightedness, or hyperopia, which affects about 5 to 10 percent of Americans.[3] It is essentially the opposite of myopia—the retina is too close to the lens. Similarly to myopia, hyperopia can also result from defects in the cornea or lens. Hyperopia causes close objects to appear blurry, while distant objects may remain in focus. It can be corrected with convex lenses (either glasses or contact lenses).

Both myopia and hyperopia can be permanently corrected through laser eye surgery. This surgery uses a high-energy beam of light to reshape the cornea. This changes the angle of light before it enters the lens, allowing light to be properly focused on the retina.

Color blindness refers to a lack of proper color perception. It is not truly a blindness. It affects men more than women: about 8 percent of men are affected by color blindness, but only 0.5

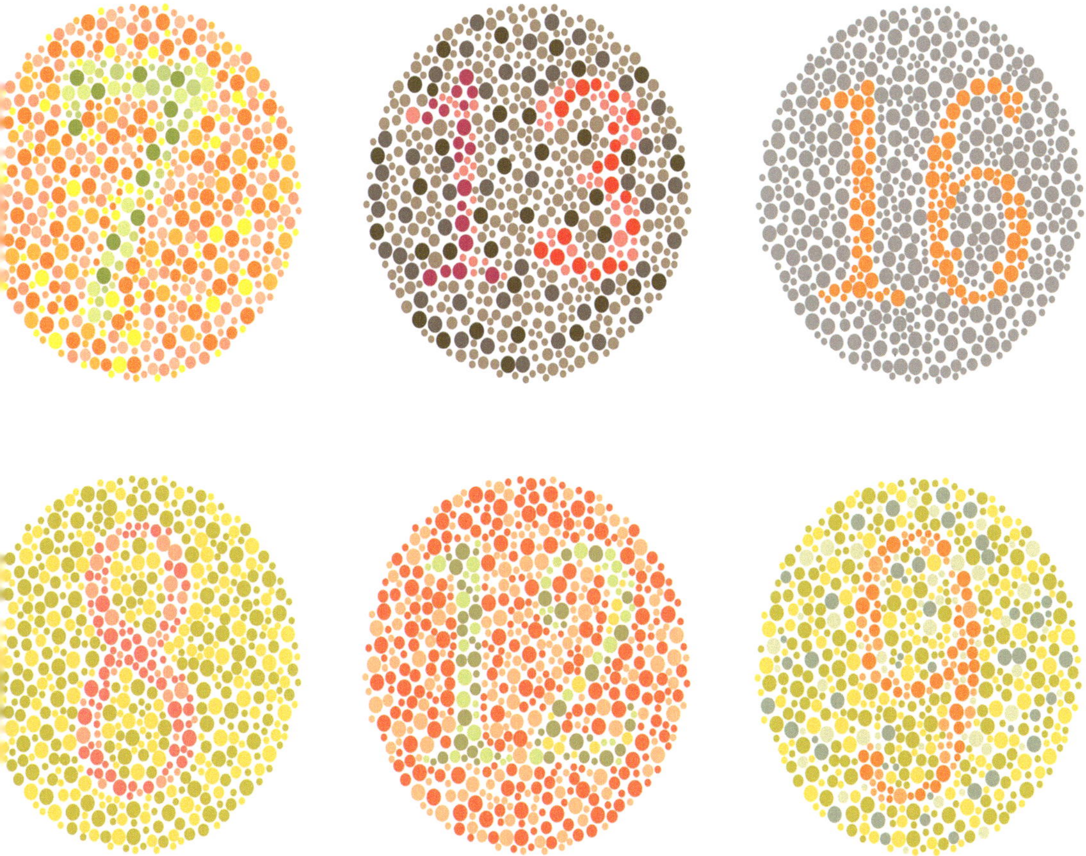

Colorblindness causes some people to have difficulty distinguishing between certain colors. Can you see all the numbers in the dots?

percent of women have it.[4] Color blindness arises from abnormal pigments—the molecules that absorb light—in the cones of the retina. Usually only a small number of colors are affected. Red-green color blindness is most common, followed by blue-yellow color blindness. Rarely, a person sees no color at all.

Blindness refers to a lack of vision. It can refer both to a complete lack of vision or to limited vision. Some people with partial blindness can detect changes in light or color. Blindness has many causes, including problems in the eye, the retina, the optic nerve, or the visual processing center of the brain. People with blindness often rely on aids to navigate, such as canes or guide animals.

Many other visual disorders also exist, such as cataracts, glaucoma, and astigmatism. Some of these can be treated or corrected, while others cannot.

Visual Filters and Enhancers

Most people are familiar with glasses and contact lenses, even when they don't wear them themselves. Concave lenses correct myopia, while convex lenses correct hyperopia.

Many people use tinted lenses, called sunglasses. This decreases the brightness of the light reaching the eye, helping people see in bright conditions. Special colors, such as yellow or orange, can also reduce glare and are often used by drivers, hunters, or anyone who has trouble seeing, especially in weather conditions like fog or rain.

When watching movies or playing some video games, some people use 3D glasses or goggles. There are a few types of 3D devices. The earliest 3D glasses used one red and one green lens. The image contained both a red and a green version, which were slightly shifted away from each other. The red lens absorbed red light but allowed green light to reach the eye, while the green lens did the opposite. This produced a 3D effect but meant

These people are wearing 3D glasses. These glasses filter light so that each eye sees a different image. The brain interprets these different images as 3D.

that the image on screen looked bizarre for anyone not wearing the glasses. Modern 3D glasses instead rely on polarization. A polarized lens blocks all light in one direction, usually either vertical or horizontal. In 3D glasses, one lens blocks vertical light, while the other blocks horizontal light. Thus, together they can produce a 3D image that still appears normal to anyone not wearing the glasses.

POLARIZED LENSES

Many sunglasses use polarized lenses. If you have ever used sunglasses with polarized lenses, you may have noticed some interesting effects. When you look at a TV or computer screen, it may look odd or be hard to see properly. The polarization makes it difficult for some of the light to get through.

If two polarized lenses are held one over the other in the same direction, they filter the same light, and you can see through them. But if one is rotated 90 degrees, they block all light!

For virtual reality (VR) and other types of gaming, 3D goggles are used. Rather than filtering certain types of light, these goggles show a unique picture to each eye. A tiny screen directs light only at the left eye, while another tiny screen directs light only at the right eye. The brain melds the inputs from each eye together to generate a whole picture with a 3D effect.

CHAPTER FIVE

NATURAL USES OF VISIBLE LIGHT

Many natural processes make use of visible light. Most light in the visible spectrum is transmitted through Earth's atmosphere, so it reaches the surface. In comparison, higher-energy wavelengths, such as gamma rays and X-rays, are absorbed by the atmosphere, as well as many lower-energy wavelengths, such as infrared.[1] Thus, most natural processes evolved to make use of light in the visible spectrum.

Photosynthesis and Plants

Perhaps the most important use of visible light that takes place on Earth is photosynthesis. Photosynthesis is the process many organisms use to transform light energy into chemical energy. In common terms, it is how living things turn light, along with water and carbon dioxide, into food. Many organisms rely on photosynthesis. Nearly all plants, as well as algae and many species of bacteria, carry out photosynthesis.

Plants use visible light in order to carry out photosynthesis. Photosynthesis also requires carbon dioxide and water.

In photosynthesis, carbon dioxide (CO_2) and water (H_2O) react through the use of light energy to produce oxygen gas (O_2) and glucose ($C_6H_{12}O_6$), a sugar. The equation can be written:

$$CO_2 + H_2O + \text{light energy} \rightarrow O_2 + C_6H_{12}O_6$$

The organism can then use this sugar as fuel for life processes, such as growth and reproduction.

The light energy used always falls in the visible spectrum. Pigments in the organism absorb specific wavelengths that cause electrons to move between molecules. A number of pigments exist, each absorbing a different set of wavelengths.[2]

Pigment	Wavelengths Absorbed
Chlorophyll a	430 nm (indigo) and 622 nm (red)
Chlorophyll b	453 nm (blue) and 642 nm (red)
Carotenoids	460–550 nm (green to yellow)

Plants rely mostly on chlorophyll a and chlorophyll b, which absorb blue and red light. This is why plants appear green—other colors of light are absorbed, while green light is reflected. Carotenoids are a class of less common pigments called accessory pigments. Carotenoids tend to appear red, orange, or yellow, as they absorb mostly green wavelengths of light.

Photosynthesis is vital to all life on Earth. First and foremost, photosynthetic organisms produce food that other organisms use. For this reason, they are called producers. Animals that eat producers are called primary consumers. Animals that eat other consumers are called secondary consumers. In this way, producers provide the energy foundation for the entire food web.

Moreover, oxygen is a product of photosynthesis. This is the mechanism by which the oxygen in the air we breathe is maintained. Humans and other animals breathe in oxygen and breathe out carbon dioxide. In this way, the matter cycles through all living things on Earth.

DARK VISION

Humans, like other mammals, see well in the dark thanks to the rods in their eyes. The ability to see in dim lighting is called "dark vision." However, bright light overwhelms the rods, and it takes time for dark vision to return.

You can see this for yourself at night. Turn off all the lights in a room, and allow three minutes to pass. Then place a hand over one eye and keep it closed, but open the other eye, and turn on the light for 30 seconds. Then, turn the light off and open both eyes. Notice a difference?

Plants also respond to changes in light. Many plants, especially some trees, lose their leaves in the fall. Although the lower fall temperatures may determine when this happens, it is also believed that the shorter periods of daylight associated with fall and winter trigger the change in these trees. In the spring, when the period of daylight lengthens again, the trees are triggered to sprout new leaves and flowers. This change in plants based on the number of daylight hours is called photoperiodism.[3]

Animal Perception

Besides photosynthesis, the other major natural use of light is animal vision perception. Humans are not the only animals who see visible light. Most animals have eyes and rely on vision as one of the senses that helps them navigate the world. We know what non-human animals can see based on the types of photoreceptors in their eyes and the pigments within those photoreceptors.

Most mammals have only two types of cones, and therefore do not distinguish between red and green. Only primates, including humans, have three types of cones. It is thought that rods evolved in mammalian eyes because mammals were once mostly nocturnal—they were active mostly at night—and vision based on rods helped them see in the dark. Only recently in mammals' evolution did the cones develop.[4]

Many non-human animals have some visual perception just outside of the visible light range. Many insects and birds can see wavelengths in the ultraviolet (UV) range. It is believed that this helps them navigate, and flowers produce intricate and beautiful patterns visible only in this range. However, these animals cannot perceive light in the red end of the visible spectrum.

Remarkably, the animal with the greatest number

Some animals can see wavelengths humans cannot. The top image shows how humans see the flower. The bottom image shows how the flower appears to animals that can see ultraviolet (UV) light.

The mantis shrimp has more photoreceptors than any other animal! Its colorful exoskeleton shows off many of the colors the shrimp can see.

of different photoreceptors is the mantis shrimp, a marine crustacean. Mantis shrimps possess a whopping twelve different kinds of photoreceptors—far more than any other animal. (In comparison, humans have three.) Researchers don't quite know what the function is of so many different photoreceptors, but they think it has something to do with pattern recognition. Mantis shrimps are brightly colored and uniquely patterned, so it's possible they use patterns of color to identify each other or to communicate.[5]

In addition to eyes, many animals have other types of photoreceptors. Even humans have photoreceptors all over their skin. This doesn't mean humans can see with their hands. Rather, the photoreceptors in skin serve to help the body understand when it is daytime and when it is nighttime. This perception helps the body know when to be awake and when to be asleep. The cycle of wakefulness and sleeping is called the circadian rhythm. Additionally, photoreceptors help protect the skin from damage. UV light, such as that from the sun, is detected by the photoreceptors in the skin. This triggers the release of skin pigment, which protects the skin and tissues beneath it from sun damage. This is why light-skinned people become tan after spending time in sunlight. However, the protection afforded by skin pigment is not perfect, so always wear sunscreen when spending time outdoors.

CHAPTER SIX

HUMAN USES OF VISIBLE LIGHT

Sight is one of the main ways humans perceive the world. As such, people have developed many uses of visible light.

Communication

Humans use light to communicate. If that is hard to believe, consider what you are doing right now. Reading a book involves light reflecting off the book and passing into the eyes. The brain interprets the difference in the colors that form the letters and processes them as words. Consider how difficult it would be to read a book if the letters were printed in white ink on white paper!

Books are not the only way humans use light to communicate, however. Nonverbal communication relies on light as well. When we have a conversation, we look at the face of the person we're talking to. The expression on their face can tell us a lot about what they're thinking.

One way humans use light to communicate is through nonverbal communication. Can you tell what this man is thinking or feeling in each image?

We also use light to communicate directly. For example, traffic lights use colored lights to signal drivers to go, use caution, or stop with green, yellow, and red lights respectively. Flashing red and blue lights indicate an emergency vehicle needs a clear path. Some ships use light to send signals to each other, using a series of flashes to spell words, similar to the way Morse code uses sound.

Light is also used in telecommunication. Optical cables transmit information in the form of pulses of light. The cables are designed specifically to transmit the light along their length so that the light that goes in one end comes out the other unchanged. Through the use of such cables, vast amounts of information can quickly be sent across extremely long distances.

Art

Humans have long relied on visible light to make art. Caves in France have been found with paintings as much as 30,000

This painting from the Chauvet Cave in France is one of the world's oldest works of art. It is between 30,000 and 33,000 years old.

years old, and even older art has been discovered. People have been using pigments from minerals, plants, and animals to paint since long before recorded history.[1]

As civilization advanced, so, too, did art. Pigments and dyes were used in paintings, fabrics, jewelry, and pottery, among other objects. Some pigments and dyes were easier to make than others. For example, the black used in many cave paintings came from the burnt remains of animals, which was readily obtainable, but other colors, such as red, were harder to be found. Red originally came from red ochre, a clay.[2]

Purple is famously associated with royalty. This is due to the extreme rarity of the purple pigment throughout much of history. Once, purple dyes were extracted from snails. Thousands of sea snails were required to obtain even one ounce of dye, which then had to be treated over the course of several days.[3] The high cost of producing purple dye led to its association with royalty, as only extremely wealthy individuals, such as kings and queens, could afford enough purple dye to color an entire garment.

Blue was also quite rare. Blue pigment is not commonly found in nature—flowers do not produce blue parts, and few stones are blue. The earliest blue pigment was achieved by mixing limestone, sand, and a copper-containing mineral such as malachite, then heating the mixture between 1,470 and 1,650 degrees Fahrenheit (800 and 900 Celsius). Later, the stone lapis lazuli was used to make blue pigment, but the rarity of the stone combined with the high cost of transforming it into pigment meant that it was incredibly expensive—pound for pound, it fetched the same price as gold. For this reason, blue became associated with holy figures, because its scarcity meant that artists reserved the color for subjects they thought deserved the highest honors.[4]

The Industrial Revolution ushered in major changes, not only in the ease of creating pigments and dyes but also in media as

Video games are a modern type of art that relies on light. The screen of your video game device emits light that your brain interprets as pictures.

well. Now, in addition to ancient forms of art such as painting, pottery, and clothing, we enjoy television, movies, and video games—all forms of art that depend on light.

One form of art that relies not just on light but on our interpretation of light is optical illusions. These are any images

This optical illusion relies on the way your brain interprets light. The colors and shapes trick your brain into thinking the picture is moving, even though it is still.

that make our brain think something is happening that is different from reality. Optical illusions rely on the ways the brain interprets light signals from the eyes. The illusions find ways to trick the brain into thinking something different is happening.

Science

A great deal of scientific discovery is based on light. In fact, an entire branch of science—optics—is devoted solely to the study of light, its properties, and its behaviors.

Yet optics alone does not encompass all the uses science has of light. Much of what we know of astronomy is thanks to the light of distant stars reaching Earth. Since ancient times, humans have been able to look into the night sky and directly observe visible light that has traveled for millions of years to reach our eyes. Today, both professional astronomers and amateurs alike point telescopes at the sky and examine the stars and planets through the use of visible light.

Other scientists, however, are less concerned with what lies beyond Earth than what lives on its surface. The light microscope, invented sometime between the sixteenth and seventeenth centuries, allows scientists to peer at the tiniest organisms.[5] The light microscope provided the foundational knowledge that led to our collective understanding of germ theory (the idea that disease is spread through contact with microorganisms), cancer, and even genetics.[6]

LIGHTING THE WAY

Some people have used light for navigation. Many anthropologists believe the Norse of the Middle Ages used a stone called a sunstone to navigate their ships. It is still unclear exactly how this worked. However, a stone called Icelandic spar is thought to be the famous sunstone. Icelandic spar notably has birefringence, which means that it splits polarized light into multiple images. By lining up the doubled images made by the stone, the Norse may have been able to locate the sun, even when it was behind clouds or below the horizon.

Lenses, Light, and Magnification

The compound microscope, in use for hundreds of years, remains quite simple in its design. It consists of a set of lenses near the eye, a set of lenses near the specimen, a light source, and a stage. The lenses near the eye focus the light so that it enters the pupil, while those near the specimen focus and magnify the light so the object can be seen. The light source provides this light, while the stage holds the specimen.

Modern microscopes have different sets of lenses for various magnification strengths, and some include a camera for taking photos of the magnified object.

Technology continues to advance. A simple light microscope, which was once a device used only by scientists on the cutting

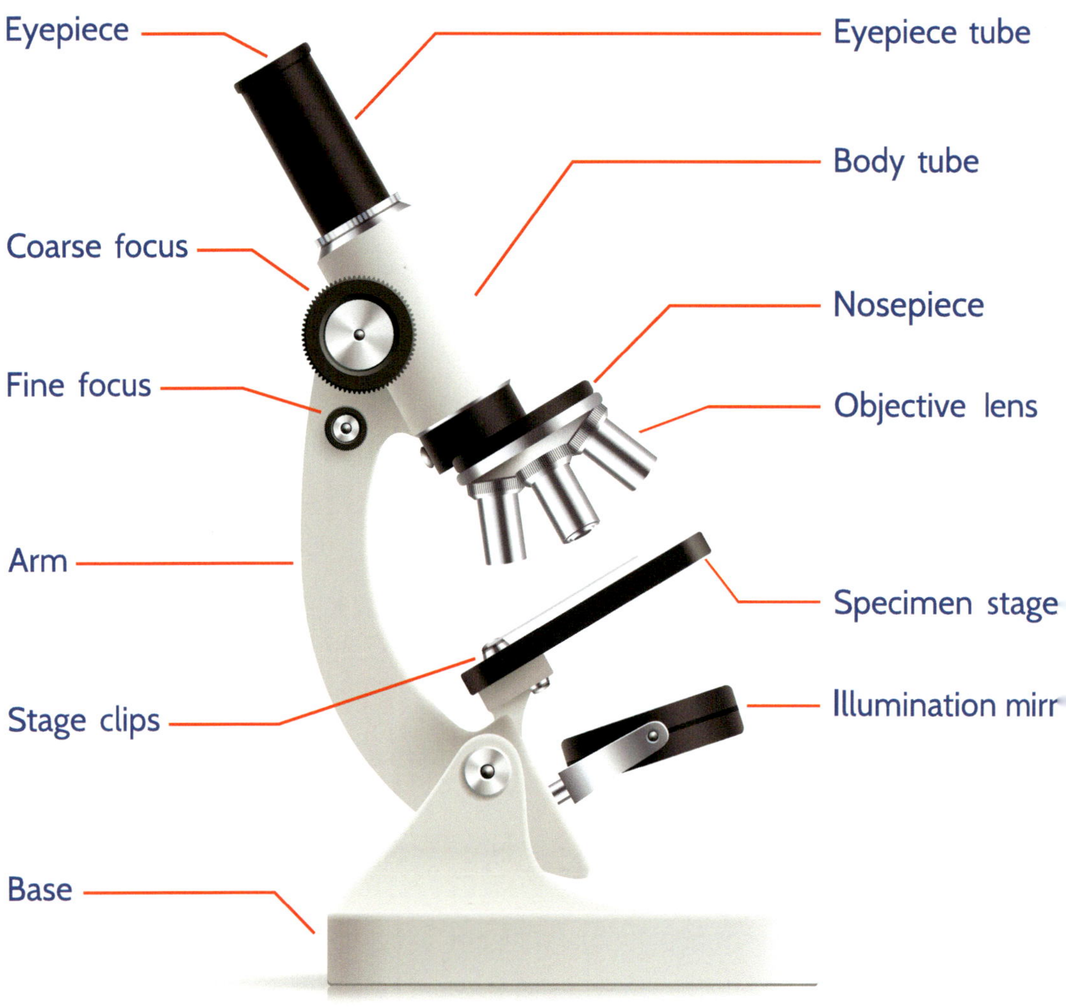

A microscope uses light to magnify objects. Microscopes can show us things that cannot be seen with the naked eye, such as cells.

edge of optics, is now available for anyone to buy for a small price. The future will certainly bring spectacular new advancements that will benefit us all.

Visible light is all around. Even in a dark room, the faint edges of objects can usually be seen. The human eyes are the product of millions of years of evolution, formed just to see this tiny fraction of the light spectrum. So next time you smile at a gorgeous sunset, gaze at the stars, or watch TV, take a moment to think about the amazing way the body uses visible light.

CHAPTER NOTES

CHAPTER 1.
THE ELECTROMAGNETIC SPECTRUM

1. National Aeronautics and Space Administration, Science Mission Directorate, "Visible Light," NASA Science, 2010, http://science.nasa.gov/ems/09_visiblelight (accessed January 18, 2019).

CHAPTER 2.
THE HISTORY OF LIGHT

1. Mohammed D. Al-Amiri, Mohamed El-Gomati, and M. Suhail Zubairy, *Optics in Our Time* (Cham, Switzerland: Springer International, 2016), p. 8.
2. Al-Amiri, El-Gomati, and Zubairy, p. 12.
3. *Encyclopedia Britannica*, online ed., "Young's Experiment."

CHAPTER 3.
THE VISIBLE SPECTRUM

1. "Colour Properties," Colour Therapy Healing, https://www.colourtherapyhealing.com/colour/colour-properties (accessed February 5, 2019).
2. *Encyclopedia Britannica*, online ed., "Reflection and Refraction."
3. Isaiah David, "How Is Light Transmitted?" Sciencing.com, updated April 24, 2017, https://sciencing.com/light-transmitted-5127127.html.
4. *Encyclopedia Britannica*, online ed., "Reflection and Refraction."

CHAPTER 4.
HUMAN PERCEPTION OF VISIBLE LIGHT

1. S. Thorpe et al., "Speed of Processing in the Human Visual System," *Nature,* volume 381, pp. 520–522 (1996), https://www.nature.com/articles/381520a0.
2. National Institutes of Health: National Eye Institute, "Facts About Myopia," https://nei.nih.gov/health/errors/myopia (accessed February 7, 2019).
3. National Institutes of Health: National Eye Institute, "Facts About Hyperopia," https://nei.nih.gov/health/errors/hyperopia (accessed February 7, 2019).
4. National Institutes of Health: National Eye Institute, "Facts About Color Blindness," https://nei.nih.gov/health/color_blindness/facts_about (accessed February 9, 2019).

CHAPTER 5.
NATURAL USES OF VISIBLE LIGHT

1. Humboldt State University, "Atmospheric Absorption and Transmission," http://gsp.humboldt.edu/OLM/Courses/GSP_216_Online/lesson2-1/atmosphere.html (accessed February 8, 2019).
2. McDaniel College, "Pigments," https://www2.mcdaniel.edu/Biology/botf99/photo/p3igments.html (accessed February 8, 2019).
3. "Photoperiodism," Biology Reference, http://www.biologyreference.com/Ph-Po/Photoperiodism.html (accessed February 13, 2019).

4. James K. Bowmaker, "Evolution of Color Vision in Vertebrates," *Eye*, pp. 541–547 (1998).
5. Stephanie Pappa, "Aggressive Mantis Shrimp Sees Color Like No Other," LiveScience, January 23, 2014, https://www.livescience.com/42797-mantis-shrimp-sees-color.html.

CHAPTER 6.
HUMAN USES OF VISIBLE LIGHT

1. Jo Marchant, "A Journey to the Oldest Cave Paintings in the World," *Smithsonian*, January 2016, https://www.smithsonianmag.com/history/journey-oldest-cave-paintings-world-180957685.
2. Jessica Stewart, "The History of the Color Red," My Modern Met, September 26, 2016, https://mymodernmet.com/shades-of-red-color-history.
3. Evan Andrews, "Why Is Purple Considered the Color of Royalty?" History.com, July 2015, https://www.history.com/news/why-is-purple-considered-the-color-of-royalty.
4. Emma Taggart, "The History of the Color Blue," My Modern Met, February 12, 2018, https://mymodernmet.com shades-of-blue-color-history/.
5. Wymke Ockenga. "A Brief History of Light Microscopy," Leica Microsystems, September 8, 2015, https://www.leica-microsystems.com/science-lab/a-brief-history-of-light-microscopy-from-the-medieval-reading-stone-to-super-resolution/.
6. Laura Poppick, "Let Us Now Praise the Invention of the Microscope," *Smithsonian*, March 30, 2017, https://www.smithsonianmag.com/science-nature/what-we-owe-to-the-invention-microscope-180962725/.

GLOSSARY

ABSORPTION The phenomenon that occurs when light interacts with the electrons of an object, causing the object itself to absorb the light energy as heat.

CONCAVE Describes the shape of a lens that is thinner in the middle and thicker on the edges. This lens can correct myopia.

CONVEX Describes the shape of a lens that is thicker in the middle and thinner on the edges. This lens can correct hyperopia.

ELECTROMAGNETIC SPECTRUM The entire range of all types of electromagnetic radiation, or light, including X-rays, ultraviolet light, visible light, infrared, and radio waves.

HYPEROPIA Farsightedness, a condition that causes close objects to appear blurry while distant objects are in focus.

LUMINOSITY Brightness, or the measurement of how much light an object emits.

MYOPIA Nearsightedness, a condition that causes distant objects to appear blurry while close objects are in focus.

OPTICS The study of light, its behaviors, and its properties.

PHOTOELECTRIC EFFECT The phenomenon of metal emitting electrons when light strikes its surface.

PHOTOPERIODISM The phenomenon that causes organisms to respond to changes in light and dark, especially referring to the loss of leaves in plants during periods of shorter daylight.

POLARIZED Describes objects, especially lenses, that block all light except those in a single direction.

REFLECTION The phenomenon that occurs when light bounces off the surface of an object rather than being absorbed or transmitted.

REFRACTION The phenomenon that occurs when light bends as it passes through an object.

TRANSMISSION The phenomenon that occurs when light passes through an object.

TRANSMITTANCE The degree to which light passes through an object.

WAVE-PARTICLE DUALITY The phenomenon of light that causes it to show properties of waves and particles, depending on the method of observation.

FURTHER READING

BOOKS

Adler, David A. *Light Waves*. New York, NY: Holiday House, 2017.

Arcand, Kimberly, and Megan Watzke. *Light: The Visible Spectrum and Beyond*. New York, NY: Black Dog & Leventhal Publishers, 2015.

Falk, David R., Dieter R. Brill, and David G. Stork. *Seeing the Light: Optics in Nature, Photography, Color, Vision, and Holography*. Brattleboro, VT: Echo Point Books & Media, 2019.

Kenny, Karen Latchana. *The Science of Color: Investigating Light*. North Mankato, MN: ABDO Publishing, 2017.

Watzke, Megan. *Light: The Visible Spectrum and Beyond.* New York, NY: Black Dog & Levanthal Publishers, 2015.

Wick, Walter. *A Ray of Light*. New York, NY: Scholastic, 2019.

WEBSITES

How Light Works

science.howstuffworks.com/light.htm

An examination of the history of discoveries about light, the physics of light and optics, and various types of natural and artificial light.

Khan Academy: Introduction to Light

www.khanacademy.org/science/chemistry/electronic-structure-of-atoms/bohr-model-hydrogen/v/introduction-to-light

A video describing light, with emphasis on understanding the physics of light.

National Aeronautics and Space Administration: Electromagnetic Spectrum Series

science.nasa.gov/ems/09_visiblelight

Take a tour of the electromagnetic spectrum.

INDEX